this way, Charlie

By

CARON LEVIS

Illustrated by

CHARLES SANTOSO

Abrams Books for Young Readers · New York

The illustrations for this book were made with digital brushes and love.

Cataloging-in-Publication Data has been applied for and may be obtained
from the Library of Congress.

ISBN 978-1-4197-4206-4

Text copyright © 2020 Caron Levis
Illustrations copyright © 2020 Charles Santoso
Book design by Pamela Notarantonio

Printed and bound in China
10 9 8 7 6 5 4

Abrams Books for Young Readers are available at special discounts when purchased in quantity for premiums
and promotions as well as fundraising or educational use. Special editions can also be created
to specification. For details, contact specialsales@abramsbooks.com or the address below.

Abrams® is a registered trademark of Harry N. Abrams, Inc.

ABRAMS The Art of Books
195 Broadway, New York, NY 10007
abramsbooks.com

For Clare and for Charles, true talents in the he**art** of friendship.
And with gratitude to all my moons.
—C.L.

For ABEL, grateful to be found, trusted, and guided
—C.S.

Jack watched the new animals scamper, hop, flap,
and trot their way into Open Bud Ranch.

Some would stay a short while, and others longer.
A few might make the ranch their home,
like Jack had when he'd needed a safe
and caring place to live.

Open Bud Ranch had space for all kinds,
and all kinds of space
to heal, rest, and grow.

Everyone could see that Jack liked
keeping his space to himself.

Everyone except Charlie.

When Charlie arrived, he didn't
see Jack at all.

"Hey!" bleated Jack.

"Pardon me!" neighed Charlie.

Jack could tell from how Charlie swerved this way
but not that way
that Charlie could only see out of one of his eyes.

Antonia explained that once in a while, for different
reasons, blindness happened.
She couldn't mend Charlie's sight
like she had the eagle's broken wing,
or release him into the wild
like the possums once they'd grown,
but she could give Charlie time to see
in his own new way.
Antonia said everybody deserves plenty of
food, love, and patience.

By now, Jack knew this ranch gave plenty of fresh hay, groomed
with soft brushes, and always trimmed hooves slowly.
Still, he didn't want anything to get
too close, too quick,
or too loud.

So Jack stepped back,
and he watched out
for Charlie.

Charlie whinnied to everyone
in a cheerful way,
swished his tail,
snorted,

and stopped to sniff
the honeysuckles,
the same way
Jack liked to.

He chewed thoughtfully
and followed the sunlit patches
as if he wanted to get to know
the whole place.

But Charlie couldn't go very far on his own.
Sometimes he bumped—
in an *oops* way, not a pushing way.
A lot of times, he stood still,
in a lost way.

Jack noticed Charlie's eye had a soft glow—
like the moon,
which often guided Jack when he felt lost in the dark.

He wondered what Charlie used for a moon.

Some mornings, Charlie pawed at a dry patch of dirt.

Scratch, scratch, scratch.

Hungry, thought Jack.

Or scared.

Maybe lonely.

One day, Jack took an extra-deep
breath of honeysuckles.
In for sweet,
out for brave.

"This way, Charlie," he said,

and showed him the way to
his favorite field.

They grazed and bathed in the sunlight.

The next day, Jack did it again.
"This way, Charlie."
Jack walked a little ahead
and on Charlie's seeing side.

He slowed down where the trail got steep,

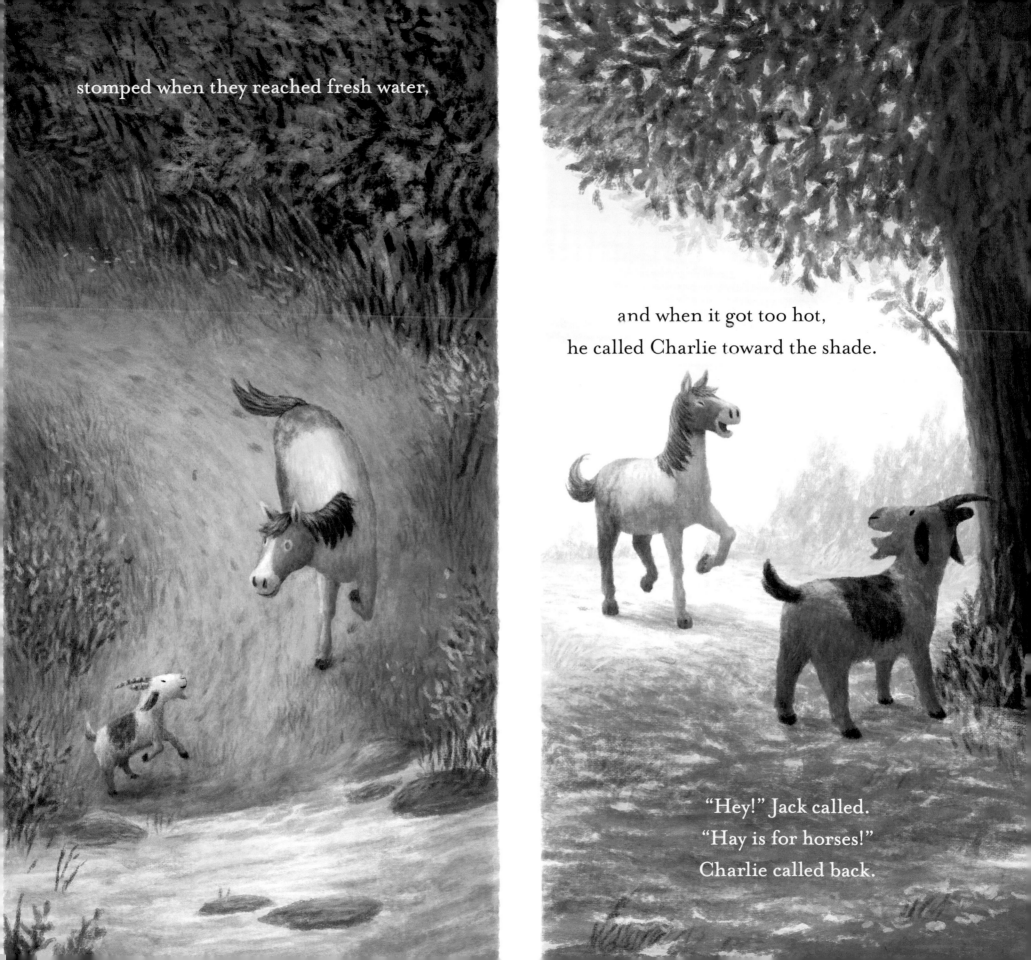

stomped when they reached fresh water,

and when it got too hot,
he called Charlie toward the shade.

"Hey!" Jack called.
"Hay is for horses!"
Charlie called back.

Soon, the next day became every day.

Walk, graze, sunbathe, return.

Sometimes, a quiet like warm milk
filled the space between them.

Other times, Jack asked Charlie questions:
about swinging a long tail,
about galloping, being so tall, going blind,
about bugs, plants, and clouds,
about the ranch, the world,
and sometimes about dreams.

"The way I see it . . ." Charlie would answer,
and Jack would listen.

On cold and wet mornings,
instead of going to their place,
Jack guided Charlie to the barn.
Charlie would step in, but Jack always stayed out.

He wanted to go where it looked peaceful and dry,
but his body remembered a different barn from
long ago that wasn't calm or kind.

Charlie couldn't make the rain or the past disappear,
but he could show Jack how kindness
moves, sounds,
and waits
for skies to clear
and new memories to take shape.

Charlie could give Jack an inside . . .

. . . outside.

Boom! Crack!

"Do you get scared of things you can't see?"
Jack asked Charlie.
"All the time," Charlie told Jack. "But the way I see it,
that's what a friend like you is for."

Friend.
Jack chewed the word over
like a mouthful of fresh, sweet grass.

As the days went by, Charlie began walking
more and more slowly.
Then, one day, he stopped.
He couldn't see out of either of his eyes now.

So Jack moved closer
and to the center of the path.

"This way, Charlie?"
"Yes, this way, Jack."

They kept walking,
one hoof in front of the other,
until it felt like Jack's steps were Charlie's,
and Charlie's steps were Jack's.

Once, when the other goats went galloping by, Charlie said, "We could play with them today." Jack trembled.

"Or maybe with the fawns?" Charlie asked. "Or the new raccoon?"

"I can't." Making new friends gave Jack a bumpy feeling.

"Let's just say hello. The way I see it—"

Charlie was surprised.
So was Jack. He hadn't meant to snap,
so close, so quick, so loud.

A new kind of quiet
filled the space between them.
It felt like a swallow of dry,
rotten grass
rumbling around their insides.

Maybe that's why they didn't notice
the sky was rumbling, too.

Boom! Crack!

Rain came pouring down so fast and thick
that Jack couldn't see Charlie.
Wind howled so loud
that Charlie couldn't hear Jack.
Trees bent, fell, and tangled—
trapping Charlie.

Jack tried this way and that way,
but there was no way in and no way out.

So Jack ran.

Jack ran and ran for Charlie.
He bleated to all the animals for Charlie.

Jack banged at doors,
found Antonia,
and urged everyone
to follow him closely.

This way! Charlie!

The mud was thick and the branches were strong,
but the whole ranch working together was stronger.

Finally, Charlie was free.
Jack led the way
inside.
"This way, friends."

Everybody huddled together.
Jack whispered, "I'm sorry."
And Charlie whispered, "Thank you."

The barn filled with all kinds
of snores, dreams,
and a quiet
that neither Charlie nor Jack could see,
but both could feel was splendid and warm,

like the sun that rose the next morning.

They walked that day, the next day,
and every day for the rest of their lives.
One hoof in front of the other.

"This way, Charlie, this way."

Author's Note

This book was inspired by the real-life relationship between Charlie the horse, Jack the goat, and their caretaker, Annette King, who founded and runs Wild Heart Ranch Wildlife Rescue and Rehabilitation Center in Claremore, Oklahoma. Wild Heart Ranch is a rehabilitate-and-release animal sanctuary where animals can get help if they are sick, hurt, or need protection. They are fed and sheltered, treated by veterinarians, and given time to heal. When they are ready, animals are released to live free in the wild or are found safe and caring homes. A few animals, like Charlie and Jack, live out their lives at the ranch.

This story is informed by the real Jack and Charlie, as well as facts about other horses, goats, and animal sanctuaries. I gathered information from videos, articles, books, and websites, then added my own experiences, observations, and imagination.

Many special human and animal friendships I have experienced or witnessed also inspired this book—and this writer. Jack and Charlie reminded me that it is both the challenges and the triumphs of friendship that help us find our way to the sunlit patches and through the rain.

—C.L.

To learn more about Wild Heart Ranch, visit wildheartrescue.org.
To explore more about the themes in this story, visit caronlevis.com.

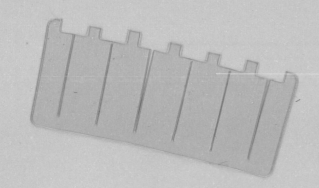